Paper Boat for Panda
published by Graffeg March 2016
Copyright © Graffeg Limited 2016
ISBN 9781910862377

Paper Boat for Panda
Text and photographs copyright © Karin Celestine
Designed and produced by Graffeg
www.graffeg.com

Graffeg Limited, 24 Stradey Park Business
Centre, Mwrwg Road, Llangennech, Llanelli,
Carmarthenshire SA14 8YP
Wales UK Tel 01554 824000
www.graffeg.com

Graffeg are hereby identified as the authors of this
work in accordance with section 77 of the Copyrights,
Designs and Patents Act 1988.

A CIP Catalogue record for this book is available from
the British Library.

1 2 3 4 5 6 7 8 9

For more fun with the Tribe visit
www.celestineandthehare.com

Celestine and the Hare
Paper Boat for Panda
by Karin Celestine

This book belongs to

GRAFFEG

Meet the Tribe

Baby Weasus was found on the doorstep on Christmas Eve and was adopted by King Norty. She is only little but clever and brave and curious with a huge kind heart. Being a weasel she is also a little bit mischievous, especially when with her daddy.

King Norty is the King of the Weasels. He can't read but uses his weaselly intelligence, wit and torrential charm for choklit snaffling. Which is what he spends his days plotting to do (along with being daddy to Baby Weasus).

Panda loves the sea and his sock hat. He likes to draw and is best friends with Emily. He is quiet and thoughtful and loves it when Emily reads to him.

Emily is wise and patient and kind and loves to read. She looks after everyone in the Shed and gives the best cuddles. She likes to make things and read books but will always stop what she is doing to hold down the knot on your parcel.

Small doesn't remember what he is or where he came from before he was found but he is small so he is called Small. He is rather quiet and shy and sometimes people don't notice him, but he is very helpful and always kind. He likes to sit in tea cups and eat biscuits and watch what is going on best of all. Everyone loves Small.

Celestine and the Hare

Karin Celestine lives in a small house in Monmouth, Wales. In her garden there is a shed and in that shed is another world. The world of Celestine and the Hare.

It is a world where weasels are ruled by King Norty, pandas ride space hoppers and bears read stories to each other. It is a place that makes people smile and where kindness is the order of the day. All are welcome.

Karin taught children, about art, about chemistry, numbers, crafts and magic, but she was always drawn back to the Shed where she brings to life creatures of all kinds using only wool, observation and the power of imagination.

Karin and the creatures love stories and kindness, books and choklit and making things, and on Sundays they have Danish pastries but not the apricot ones because they are frankly wrong.

Celestine, her great grandmother and namesake, watches over all in the shed and the hare sits with her; old wisdom helping the Tribe along their path in life.

Celestine and the Hare
Paper Boat for Panda

For my mother Anne Karin who wove
the rug to look like the sea.

Panda loves the sea. Every year
he goes on holiday to the seaside.
There is a toy boat there.
He loves to sail the boat on the kitchen
rug that was made to look like the sea.
Sometimes he sits up and rows.

Sometimes Panda likes to
ruckle up the rug to make
waves. Then he sits in the
bottom of the boat and sails the
stormy, high-rug seas.

Panda tells Baby Weasus stories of
sailors and pirates and how he would like,
just once, to sail on the sea for real.
But he knows his boat is just a toy
and would sink on any sea but the
rug sea. So it is just a dream.

One beautiful evening the sea was as smooth as glass. Panda was sitting on the jetty looking longingly out to sea. Baby Weasus saw him wishing and had an idea. She ran into the house.

Baby Weasus found some old rolls of wallpaper in the cupboard. She chose yellow because it is a happy colour and she cut a big piece. With Small's help, she started to fold the paper.
They folded...

...and folded and folded.
Sometimes they had to jump on it.
When they were done she hugged Small thank you and ran outside to find Panda.

She found Panda still sitting by the sea,
lost in dreams.
She gently tapped him on the shoulder
because you should always be gentle
with dreamers.
She asked him to come with her as she
had a surprise for him.

'I made you a paper boat, Panda! Small
helped too. It will float for this evening
while the sea is soft and smooth and still.
I found a feather and put it in the
front for you too, to make it extra pretty.'
Panda was so happy he started to cry.

Panda could not believe how beautiful his boat was. He hugged Baby Weasus and found a salt-caked goose feather on the shore and put it as a mast. Then he set sail for the wide and beautiful sea while Baby Weasus waved him off.

He sailed and he sailed and he sailed
on the glass-smooth sea,

and he sailed until the sun had set and
the moon shone silver sparkles.

Panda would never forget the night
he got to sail on the real sea.
'Thank you, Baby Weasus, my dear friend.'

How to make a paper boat

You can make your own paper boat. Baby Weasus and Small will show you how.

Get a rectangle of any paper you like. It can be plain or coloured. This piece was A4 size but it doesn't matter what size, you just get a tiny or a huge boat.

Fold it in half so the folded edge is at the top. If you have coloured paper, the top side here will be the colour of the sail and the inside the colour of the boat sides.

Once folded in half, make a crease in the
centre so you know where to fold to next.

Fold the corners into the middle
to make a triangle.

Lift up one of the bottom flaps and fold against the bottom of the triangle.

Fold the little triangles sticking out
around the back like like Baby Weasus
has done. Small needs to do his side now.

Hurrah, Small has done it!
They look the same now.

Now, you can turn the paper over to
see what the back looks like.

Fold up the flap against the triangle
like the other side...

...and fold the triangles around
the back, same as before.

Open up the shape you have now
got like a hat. It's a bit big for Small!

Once open, pull the two corners
together like you are making a bird's
beak so it becomes a square. You can
take a moment to flap it open and
shut a bit and say 'hello' if you want.
Then press it flat. Baby Weasus and
Small have to jump on it to make it
go flat. You can probably just press.

It should look something
like this now.

Next fold up the triangles on the front and back. If you fold them not quite so high, it makes the sail bigger. You can experiment and see what you like best.

Then you do the 'opening up funny bird beak' folding the corners the other way again to make another square.

Jump on it to make it flat.

It should look a little bit like this, but
if you did the triangles all the way up,
you won't see any of the inner part.
That's fine.

44

Now you hold it up and do the magic bit. Hold one of the top corners in each hand and start to pull apart.

It should pop out into a boat shape.

Open up underneath inside the sail a
bit to make it more stable.

47

Hurrah! You now have a boat.
You can colour it in or decorate it
any way you want.

You can colour in your boat or use
patterned paper. Panda likes to use old
maps for his. You could add a Viking
dragon head to it, or a flag, or you could
write a sekrit wish in the folds that
no one can see and set them free on
the sea or down a river. You can make
small people from paper or acorns to
sail your boat, or make a bigger boat
for your teddy. They will float for a
short time in water (longer if you rub
them with wax crayon or a candle) or
you could thread them into a mobile.
Or just put one on your shelf by your
bed and dream of sailing the high seas
like Panda.